I0527116

Copyright © 2018 by Aaron Thayer
Illustrations by Charity Russell

All rights reserved. This book or any portion thereof may not
be reproduced or used in any manner whatsoever without
the express written permission of Thayer Family Books LLC
except for the use of brief quotations in a book review.
Printed in the United States of America

First Printing, 2018

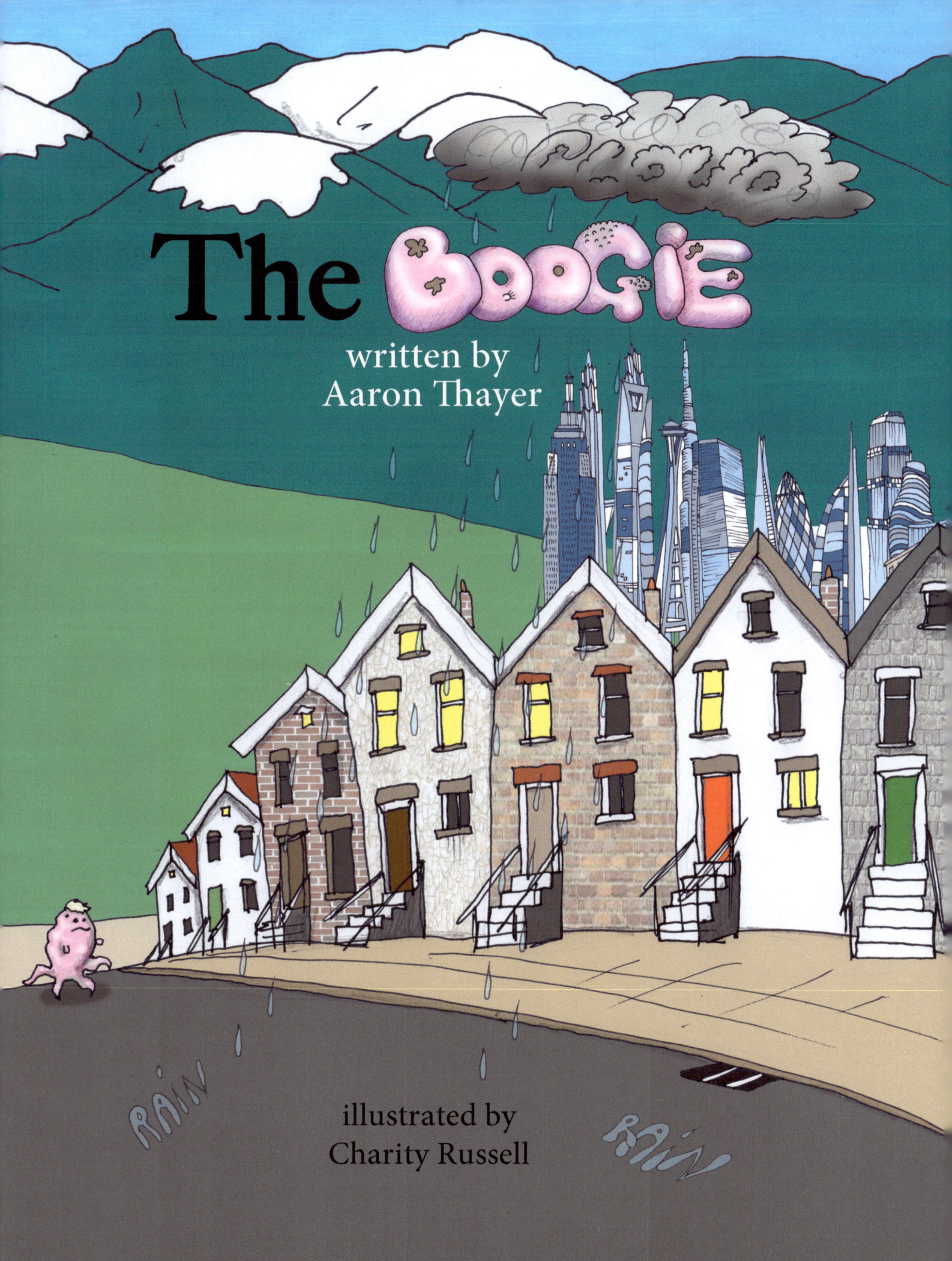

In the land of Goz the Boogie lived,
eating words to stop each kid
from learning about the world that was,
and the world that is,
and the greatness of Goz.

The Boogie ate words it thought were delish.
Delish to the max, like Soft and Swish.
And once they were eaten, no kid would know,
that the words ever existed, either now or ago!

Luiza lived in Goz
and slept in her bed,
but when Boogie ate "Soft"
her pillows turned lead.

8

Greg lived in Goz too
and liked to sleep in.
One day he woke up,

his "Swish" hair had turned thin!

9

First the Boogie ate slow,
and all seemed the same,
but a Sunday came that saw changes
to all sorts of names.

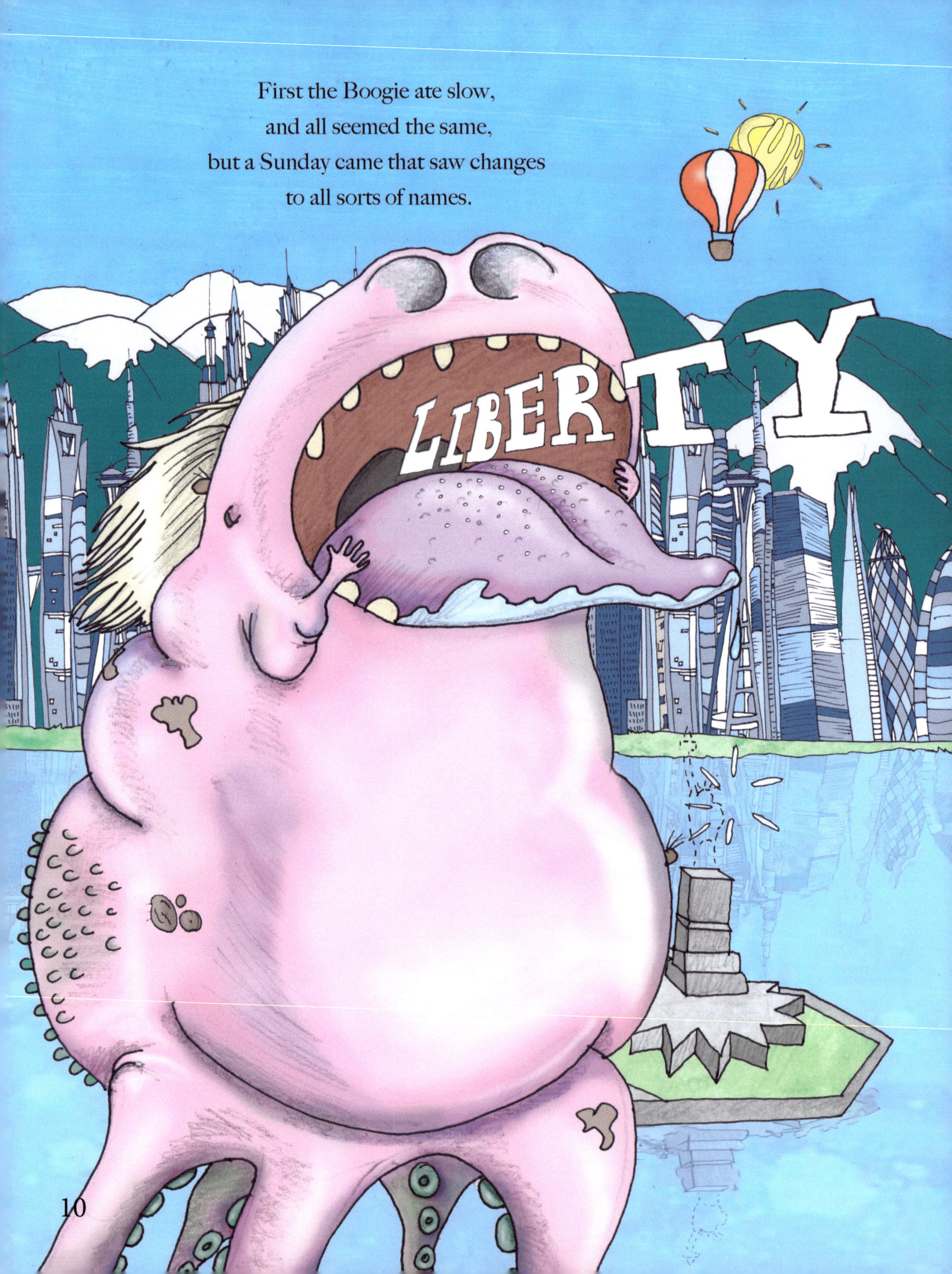

Luiza and Greg walked out the next day...
some things were missing, though
exactly what,
they could not say.

11

They boarded a bus to take them some place.
But the place was all different -
the space was erased.

Their backpacks had gone,

disappeared into thin air,

the kids got off the bus,

but the school was no longer there!

Uncle Mac in his truck was parked there instead.

He sold sweets to the kids, with thin hair and hard beds.

For Uncle Mac knew, the kids would want treats.

(All too easy exchanging books for things that are

sweet!) The two friends did just that,

ordered ice cream post haste!

What a deal! No learning!

What great things
to taste!

Then something happened,
their ice cream turned warm.
The air it did too,
and Mac's freezer changed form.
Then the cream disappeared
and Greg looked at his cone,
and Luiza did too
and boy did they moan!

15

"It's the Boogie!" said Mac.
"He's eating my words!
That building was fine -
since it was absurd."

16

"But desserts are delish and delish should be sold.
We must turn this around, it is time to be bold!"

Mac, Greg and Luiza,
they led all the kids,
they followed the lettered trail
to where Boogie lived.

"**oh** that's a surprise," said Greg,
and Luiza agreed.
It wasn't a cave, but a house,
white indeed.

18

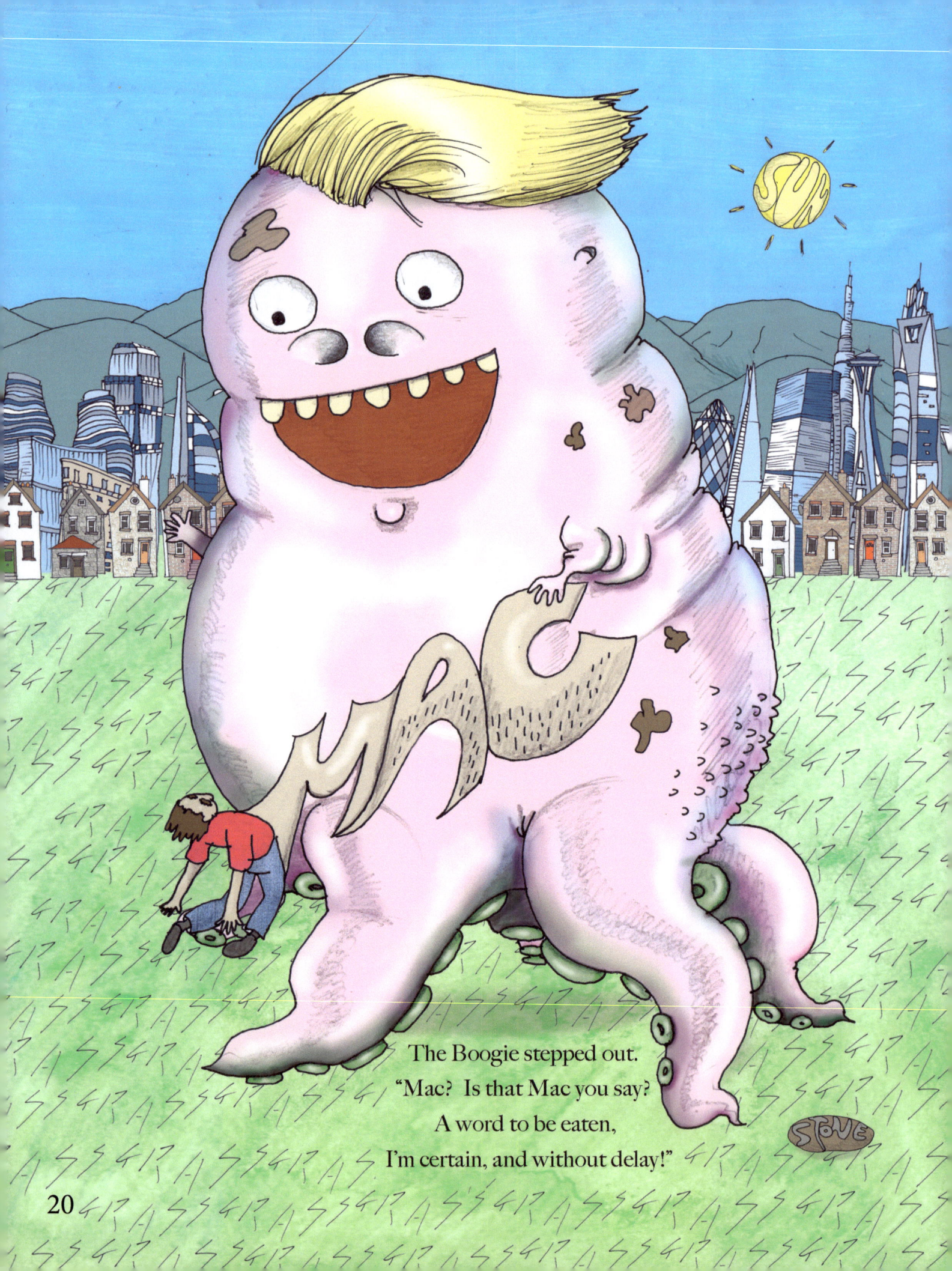

The Boogie stepped out.
"Mac? Is that Mac you say?
A word to be eaten,
I'm certain, and without delay!"

20

"He's a person!" cried out Greg.
"Oh who cares?" Boogie said.
"Then these first," shouted Luiza,
"For I've got quite the spread."

21

Chocolate milkshakes candy

Luiza tossed up chocolate,
and there went up a cry,
and then milkshakes,
and candy, and tart lemon pie.

TART LEMON PIE

22

The kids were all saddened
and the Boogie grew large,
but it also grew sick,
and looked to discharge.

23

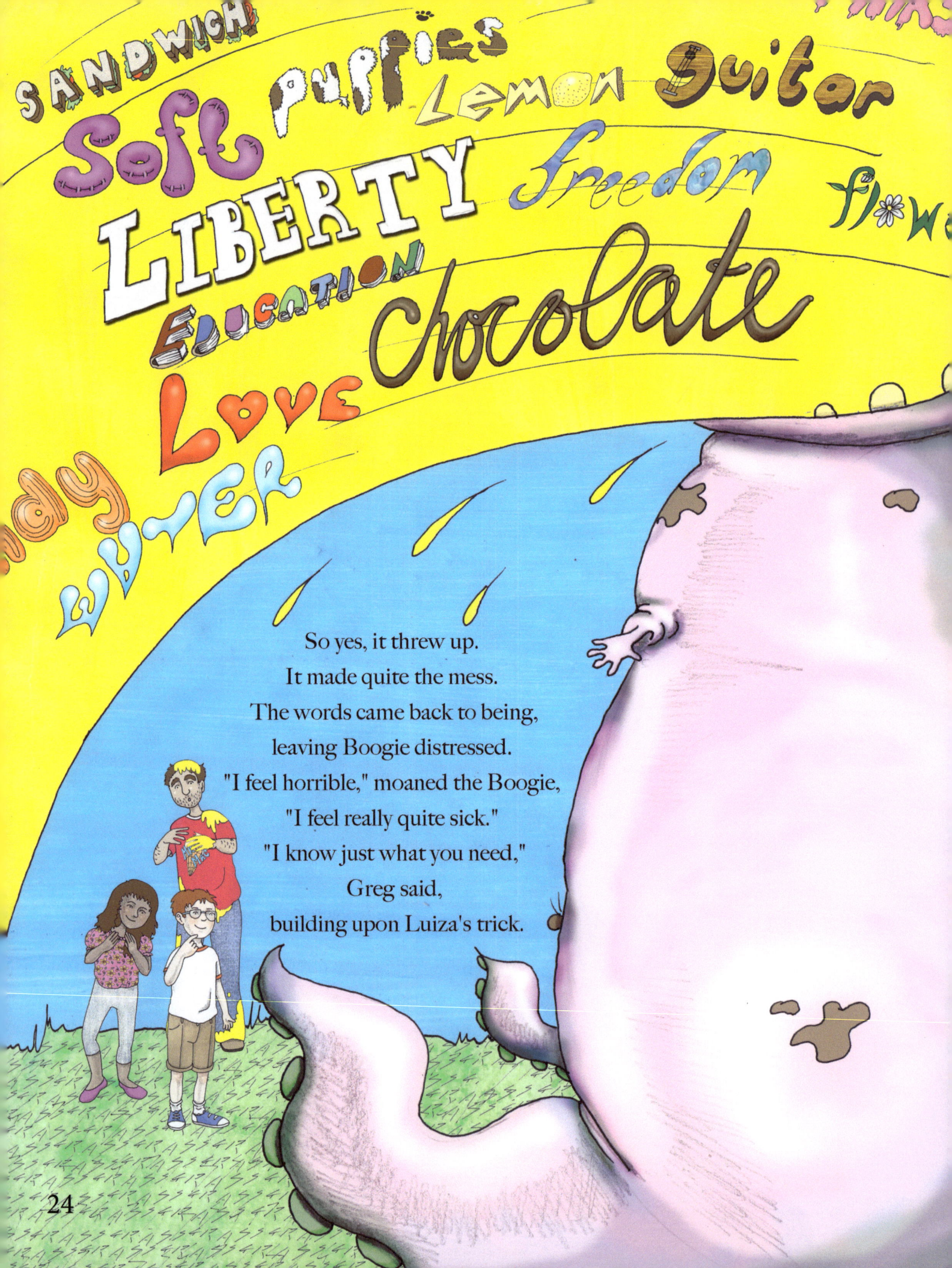

So yes, it threw up.
It made quite the mess.
The words came back to being,
leaving Boogie distressed.
"I feel horrible," moaned the Boogie,
"I feel really quite sick."
"I know just what you need,"
Greg said,
building upon Luiza's trick.

24

As the Boogie chomped down
the one word that would feed,
feed that ego of Boogie's,
the Boogie's one true deep need.
Their eyes were all wide,
for the word that Greg threw,
was the very word Boogie...

25

Luiza and Greg, they had ice cream again.

And they went back to school!

Yet every now and then...

They would dream deeply, see visions,
and wake with a start.
They knew in the future, they would again play their part.

The Boogie: A Thayer Family Story

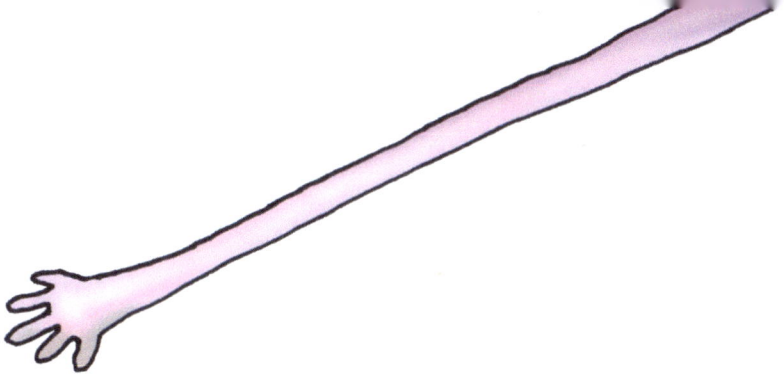

Friends make it easier to stand up to Boogies.

www.ingramcontent.com/pod-product-compliance
Lightning Source LLC
Chambersburg PA
CBHW041543240626

47164CB00002B/111